Lion

Pig

Lobster

Kangaroo

Eagle

Chimpanzee

cat

Turtle

Dog

Baboon

Fish

Tiger

Hedgehog

Kiwi

Parrot

Stag Beetle

Anteater

chicken

Budgie

orangutan

Rhino

Bat

Squirrel

Donkey

Toad

Owl

crab

Dolphin

cow

Rat

Seal

Tortoise

camel

Ant

Peacock

Jellyfish

otter

Zebra

Snail

Chameleon

Rabbit

Sheep

Panda

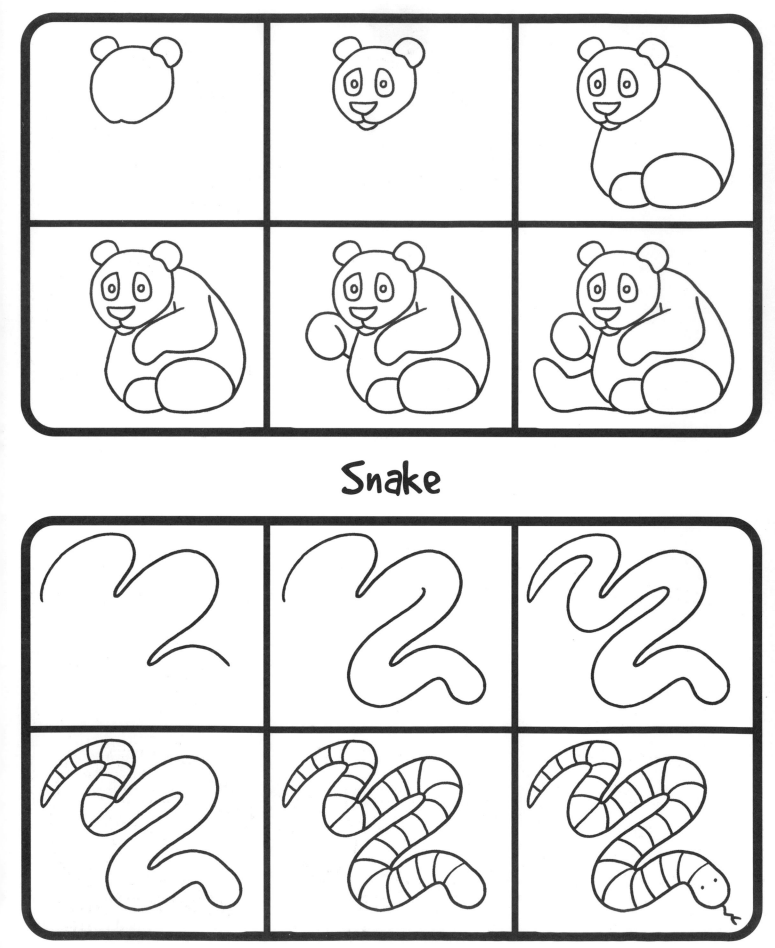

Snake

Killer Whale

Toucan

Lemur

Bison

Horse

Penguin

Elephant

Frog

Shark

Goat

Panther

Kingfisher

Grasshopper

Squid

Duck

Porcupine

Humpback whale

Beaver

Koala

Walrus

Spider

Mouse

Flamingo

Bear

Sloth

Hippo

Buffalo

Dragonfly

Cheetah

Shrimp

Monkey

Heron

Puffin

Armadillo

Octopus

Bee

ostrich

Gorilla

cuttlefish

Ladybug

Swan

Manta Ray

Blue whale

Crocodile

Worm

Wolf

Mole

Angler fish

Starfish

Polar Bear

Hammerhead Shark

House Fly

Woodpecker

Sperm Whale

Angel fish

Cobra

Butterfly